Pizza Soup

By Fay Robinson
Illustrations by Ann Iosa

 CHILDRENS PRESS®

CHICAGO

Library of Congress Cataloging-in-Publication Data

Robinson, Fay.
  Pizza soup / by Fay Robinson : illustrated by Ann W. Iosa.
    p. cm. — (Bear and alligator tales)
  Summary: As her toys, Bear and Alligator, watch, Nicki and her father plan,
shop, and prepare a special dinner. Includes recipe.
  ISBN 0-516-02373-X
  [1. Cookery—Fiction. 2. Fathers and daughters—Fiction. 3. Toys—Fiction.
4. Stories in rhyme. 5. Cartoons and comics.] I. Iosa, Ann, ill. II. Title. III. Series:
  Robinson, Fay. Bear and alligator tales.
PZ8.3.R57Pi 1992
[E]—dc20   92-10756
                                                                CIP
                                                                 AC

5

7

9

10

11

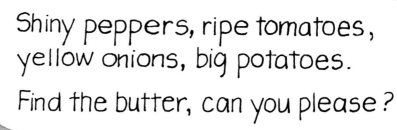

12

DAIRY →

Sale
59¢

13

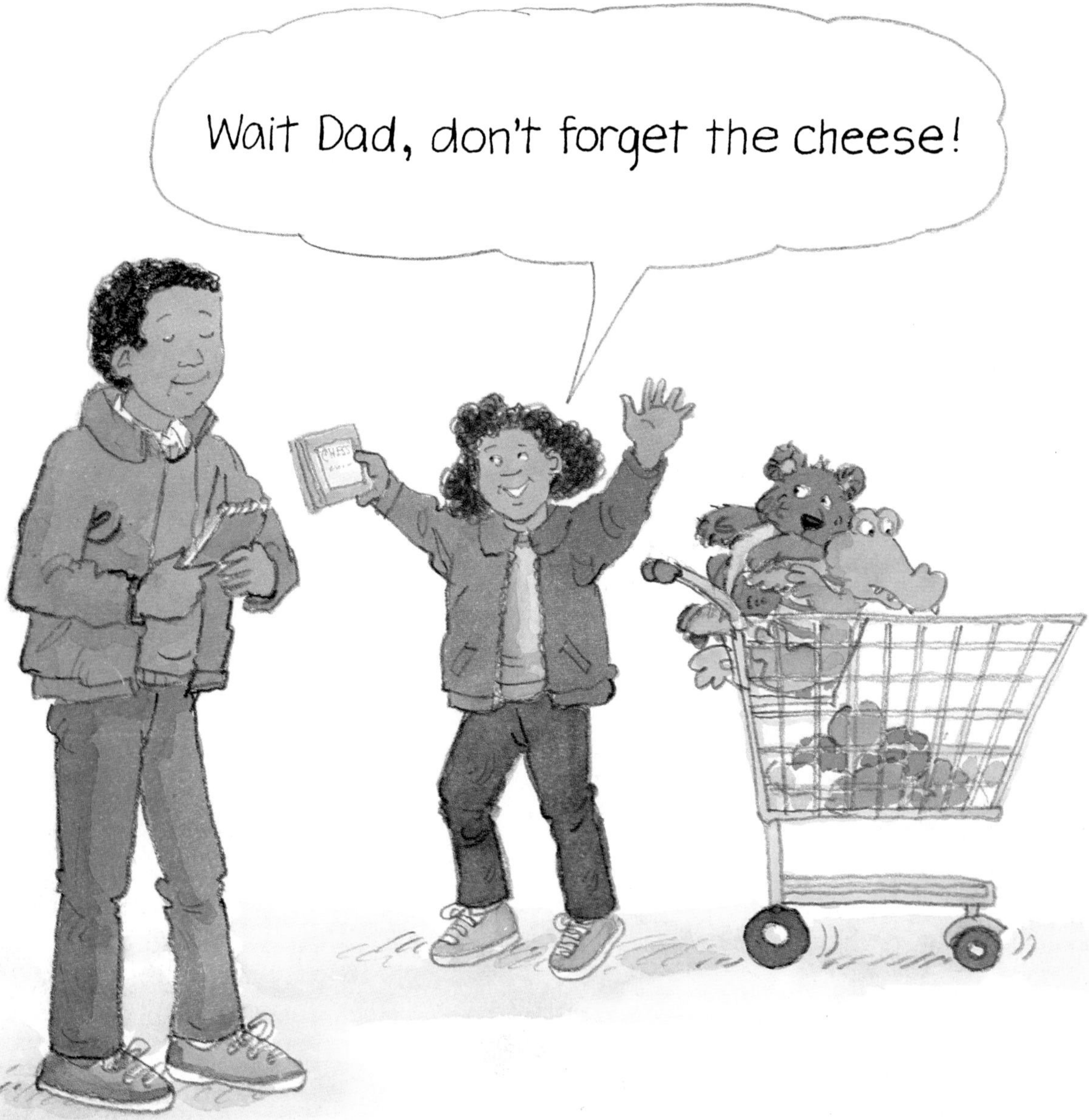
Wait Dad, don't forget the cheese!

15

16

20

21

22

27

28

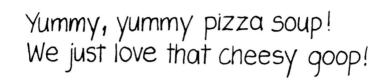

Recipe for Pizza Soup
(Makes soup for four to six people)

You will need:
a grown-up to use sharp knives and the stove
1 green pepper
1 yellow onion
1 potato
3 large tomatoes
3 tablespoons butter or margarine
4 cups water
½ teaspoon oregano
⅛ teaspoon powdered garlic
sliced mozzarella cheese
sliced French bread

1. Wash the pepper, potato, and tomatoes, and take the brown skin off the onion. Cut them all into bite-sized pieces. Put the pieces into a large pot.
2. Add the butter and cook for five minutes.
3. Add the water, oregano, and garlic powder. Cook on low heat for one hour.
4. Put a slice of bread into each bowl.
5. Pour soup over the bread, covering it.
6. Put a slice of cheese on top. Let it melt for two minutes.
7. Eat your soup!